Winter Tales
of the
Snowbabies©

Department 56® INC.

ISBN 0-9622603-4-7

Printed in the United States
First printing June 1995
10 9 8 7 6 5 4 3

Winter Tales
of the
Snowbabies©

Snowbabies created by
Kristi Jensen Pierro and Bill Kirchner

Written by
Carolyn M. Johnson

Illustrated by
Kirsten Soderlind

Published by
Department 56

*O*nce upon a time . . .
In a far off wintry land
Jack Frost grew lonely
And took the task to hand.
He used his magic powers
And smiled when he was through,
For what he'd made were Snowbabies
A joy for me and you.

*O*n tiny sleds they slide
Down icy hills they go
They laugh and sing together
As they frolic in the snow.
And while they're busy playing
Throughout the frosty day
They hope the winter sunshine
Won't melt them all away.

A Long-Forgotten Legend

In a long-forgotten legend from a time so long ago, when the magic of the four seasons first began, it was written that after three seasons had passed, when all the leaves had fallen from the trees, Autumn glanced over her shoulder and was gone. Then all the earth grew hushed and still, and the days grew shorter, and the midnight sky was filled with stars.

And as the last bright leaf clung to its branch, the Old North Wind began to blow. He circled and twirled in the frosty night, singing his winter song. Until at last his song reached the highest mountain peak, where deep in an ice cave, it woke the sleeping Jack Frost.

Jack Frost yawned and stretched and opened his eyes, where a twinkle appeared. He shook his head, and the icicle curls of his long beard jangled like bells. He lifted his long arms and smoothed the folds of his great snowcape, then peered out across the land, over the hills, the valleys, rivers, and mountains.

Jack Frost sighed, for he saw that Autumn and her magical colors were gone. Now all the land lay frozen and glossed, silent and still. He grew melancholy, for he wished that the first snowfall would begin to fill the empty air. He waited . . . a few snowflakes began to fall. Then more and more fell, and as Jack Frost looked up, a smile crossed his face.

He billowed his snowcape wide and raised his starwand high, and in a burst of wintry magic, stardust filled the air. And from each tiny starspark tiny Snowbabies appeared, drifting lightly onto the snowflakes which were falling throughout the world. And so was born the legend of the Snowbabies.

Frosty Frolic Land

*L*ook up when the earth is freshly frosted with the first touch of snow. Reach out and let a snowflake settle gently on your mitten. Is it a snowflake? Only a snowflake? Or could this be the tiny world where the Snowbabies live?

To any of us, a snowflake appears quite small. But to the Snowbabies, it is a vast and wintry Frosty Frolic Land. A magical land, thick with starry pine forests, glistening with frosty lakes, surrounded by towering snow-covered mountains. A sparkling land, from the cascading waterfalls to the rivers winding like silver ribbons to the shores of the starry sea.

At first glance, this tiny snowflake land might appear serene and uninhabited. But on a closer look, you'll discover a magical, bustling world where each day the Snowbabies, clad in their frosty suits, tumble from their icy igloos built on the banks of sparkling rivers. They romp throughout their busy days, searching for stars and frolicking merrily in the snow. There, they are eagerly joined, whether at work or at play, by their animal friends.

Together with the kind polar bear, the wise walrus, the puffins, and the penguins, the Snowbabies gather the stars and play follow the leader . . . or hide-and-seek . . . or join in a parade!

So, next time the snow falls, look more closely at each snowflake. For you'll find that, no matter the task, whatever the game, the inhabitants of this tiny world are always there for you to see.

A Winter's Gift

On a frost-tipped morn in a wintry land
A little girl stretched out a mittened hand,

And the glistening snowflakes which filled the air
Fell on her boots, her coat, and her hair.

They fell on her mitten,
    where to her surprise,
She discovered a world
    just snowflake size.
The little girl blinked—
    there was no mistake!—
Tiny Snowbabies lived on
    each tiny snowflake.

Clad in their snowy suits, eyes twinkling brightly,
Dimpled and laughing as snow drifted lightly,
The Snowbabies tumbled and played the long day
And gathered the stars from the wide Milky Way.

$\mathcal{T}$hen as the star-gatherers drew in their treasure,
A few more from here and from there for good measure,

And scattered the starshine all over The Pole,
How their snowworld did sparkle from valley to knoll!

Such loveliness called for a great celebration,
And the Snowbabies started their glad preparation.
To the far Frosty Forest by the deep starry sea,
They traveled in search of the right Christmas tree.

$\mathcal{T}$he snowfriends went wandering the winter woods round
Until deep in a thicket a proud pine they found.
Such wondrous things hung from its snow-dusted limbs,
The whole tree was wreathed in a wealth of bright trims!

Amid glittering star garlands gracefully hung,
There were hidden surprises with white ribbon strung.
A shining brass bugle, a clear silver bell,
There were cymbals and drums and a toy flute, as well.

There were boxes and bundles untold to unwrap,
There were mittens and mufflers—no time for a nap!
A fine pair of ice skates, a new pair of skis,
Were there ever more wonderful presents than these?

Yet some puzzling questions remained in the air—
Where did they come from? Did Jack Frost leave them there?

Then what frolic and fun round the star-sparkled tree,
As delightful a dance as you ever did see!
Until all joined together in a grand promenade
Of friendship and gladness, a Christmas parade.

And the tinkling music now spread far and near,
Proclaiming the joyous news,

CHRISTMAS
IS HERE!

The sounds of such merriment soon reached the place
Where Jack Frost kept watch, and a smile crossed his face.
He would give all a gift; then he winked a wise eye,
And a rainbow of light crossed the midnight sky.

The stars grew more brilliant, the colors entwined,
And his magical gift shone on all humankind,
With nothing expected, no thought of return,
A gift given freely—a lesson to learn?

When the little girl gazed from her window that night
At the Christmas aurora and the bright starry light,
She knew in her heart that as long as you live,
The best present of all is the one that you give.

You Didn't Forget Me

With so many things
To remember and do,
You didn't forget me,
And I didn't forget you.

Are These All Mine?

I can count two, three, four,
Seven, eight, nine.
Are these for you, or
Are these all mine?

Why Don't You Talk to Me?

Why don't you play with me,
Spend the whole day with me?
Why don't you dance with me?
Come take a bow!
Come take a chance with me!
Why don't you answer me?
Why don't you talk to me?
Don't you know how?

A Winter's Journey

The bright winter days, how they glimmered and gleamed
As the sparkling snow fell. And the little girl dreamed
That she lived with the Snowbabies all the long day
On the dancing snowflakes, where she joined in their play.

*T*hen, one frosty morning she opened her door
To a snowfall more radiant than ever before.

She pulled on her mittens and dashed down the stair
In search of the Snowfriends. But, they were not there!

*N*ow, the Snowbabies, too, had awoke to the sight
Of the shining surprise which had come in the night.
For a glistening frost blanket covered the land,
Why, The Pole was a white wintry wonderland!

There were rivers and forests, meadows and mountains,
Cascading waterfalls, ice-crystal fountains.
From high land to low, all was frozen and glossed.
Who could have done this? Was it Jack Frost?

A journey was planned, they would travel and find
The one who had left such enchantment behind.
They would find him and thank him, for one and for all,
Who loved his frost magic, both big folk and small.

The Snowbabies took up
    their snowshoes and packs
For gathering the stars,
    which they wore on their backs.

On skates, skis, and sleds—some on wingtip, no less—
They started their journey—on the Polar Express!

On a bridge of bright stars, 'cross the great Milky Way,
On a kind polar bear, a toboggan, a sleigh,

O'er the wide starry sea in a frosty dream boat,
The Snowbabies wandered, aloft and afloat.
While the puffins were patiently starfishing, too,
And a walrus watched wisely from his point of view,
They searched near and far, in the air, on the ground,
But the one they were searching for couldn't be found.

$\mathcal{T}$he travelers grew weary, at last, of their quest,
And as night fell, their thoughts turned to homeland and rest.
And the stardust they'd strewn throughout forest and glen
Was the starpath they followed back homeward again.

Now, who should be watching the friends' caravan,
As it wound its way back to the place it began?
With his long flowing beard and his clear twinkling eyes,
'Twas Jack Frost himself, who had one last surprise.

With a wink and a wave of his starwand on high,
A silvery snow filled the wide midnight sky.
It fell through the darkness and gathered the light
Of the moon and the stars, and it lit up the night,

Until those who had set out, the wide world to roam,
Were safely returned, were once again home.
And on into morning the bright snowshine fell,
And held all The Pole in its magical spell.

THE POLE

The little girl smiled while the snowflakes swirled,
As she watched from the door of her own cozy world.
And she thought of the Snowbabies' journey, then guessed,
Although we love traveling, we love home the best.

I'm Right Behind You

Lead and I'll follow,
Hide and I'll find you.
'Cross hill or hollow.
I'm right behind you.

Winken, Blinken, and Nod

Rocking along on the moonbright sea,
While the waves hum a moonlight melody,
Fishing for dreams go the starfishers three,
Winken, Blinken, and Nod . . . that's me!

A World of Good Friends

In the magical world of the Snowbabies, each of their animal friends has its own special task.

The kind polar bear leads the way on expeditions. Whenever the Snowfriends go off on an adventure, he is there to watch over them with his great strength and patience, and they trust that he will lead them safely home again.

The wise walrus knows many things. He can ponder great questions, consider important issues, solve complicated riddles. His Snowbaby friends look to him for guidance and wisdom.

The quick and frisky rabbit is an expert at getting in and out of tight places. He burrows deep into snowdrifts, beneath low-hanging pine boughs, behind thick icicle curtains and finds hidden stars, which he points out to the Snowbabies, who load them into their brimming baskets and packs.

The helpful puffins are always happy to assist when there's starfishing to be done. Or look on when a new icy igloo is built.

And, of course, the playful penguins are ever about, curious and inquisitive, silly and brave, always mischievous. And their friends, the Snowbabies, love them best of all.

The Snowbabies, in turn, provide the fun and the celebration, the games and the glee throughout the holiday season, which keep all of the inhabitants of this magical snowworld filled with the merriment and gladness only true friendship can bring.

The Polar Express

We're going somewhere,
You'll never guess.
How will we get there?
The Polar Express.

Who Are You?

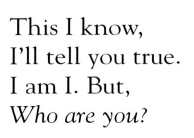

This I know,
I'll tell you true.
I am I. But,
Who are you?

The Magic of Bright Stars

When frost laces the wide world on a winter's morning and the air glistens with snow, the Snowbabies are getting ready for another day of gathering stars. All across The Pole they don backpacks and take up ice skates, sleds, and skis. While some cross the slippery slopes on tiny toboggans and others catch the breeze in frosty boats, the Snowbabies scatter far across Frolic Land in search of stars.

Up hill and down, through forest and field, over rivers, around mountains, they make their way. Here, a star hides behind a starry pine! There, another peeks from beneath a dancing cloud! Soon their backpacks are filled and brimming, their sleighs and sleds, sacks and satchels, are glowing and overflowing with stars. Then the Snowbabies turn toward home with their shining treasures.

Now, some of you might wonder, why are the Snowbabies always looking for stars? Why do they gather them? And what do they do with them?

To begin with, when a star in the night sky no longer shines—yes, that does happen—the Snowbabies replace the old star with a new one, so it can twinkle and shine once again. And, during holiday celebrations, the Snowbabies hang their stars as bright decorations on the towering pines in the Frosty Forest.

And last but not least, the Snowbabies love most of all to give their stars away to one another. And though no one knows for sure— for the Snowbabies will not tell—it is believed these stargifts are what make the snowflakes glisten. Step outside on a winter's eve and discover this magic for yourself.

A Winter's Celebration

The winter wind blew and the snowflakes pranced,
And the icicles grew and the snowshadows danced.

And up in her room at the top of the stair,
With gaily wrapped packages piled everywhere,
The little girl sat amid ribbons and bows,
Surrounded by presents she carefully chose.
For this magic time she had waited all year,
Tomorrow was Christmas! It soon would be here!

In Frolic Land, also, the merriment grew,
For the Snowbabies waited for Christmas Day, too!
They'd hustled and bustled and were ready at last,
Only one task remained. They would have to work fast!

*I*n satiny starnets tossed high as the moon,
While the North Wind whistled a wintry tune,

In starbaskets brimming with silvery store,
They collected the stars, and went looking for more.
Cloud castles, treetops, a star couldn't hide,
No matter the place, but oh, how they tried!

Beyond the blue sea and the mountains so white,
The Snowbabies searched, all the day, all the night.

They pulled in the stars from the ends of the sky,
And whisked the stars home in the wink of an eye,
They wrapped them with bright ribbons trailing behind,
And hid them well, for one another to find.

*N*ow, this year the Snowfriends
    had thought of a plan,
For their old friend Jack Frost.
    They'd make one star so grand,
It would outshine the rest,
    and he'd see it and know,
It was their gift to him
    for his gift of the snow.

So they gathered the leftover stars into one,
The most radiant of all! And when they were done,
The great star shone down upon all Frolic Land,
As if to say, Christmas! It's finally at hand!

And the secret is this, in the Snowbabies' story,
They celebrate friendship in gladness and glory!
For though they love stars, what they love most of all,
Is giving the stars to their friends, great and small.

*A*nd these stargifts, how brightly they shimmer and shine!
How they sparkle the snowflakes, in your world and mine!
And remind us, whenever snow glistens the air,
That good things get better with someone to share.

Now, the little girl had a fine Christmas, it's true,
She gave away presents, and opened some, too.
And the pile of gifts grew by the tall Christmas tree.
But something was missing. What could it be?

When no one was watching, she reached far inside
The toe of her stocking, and her eyes opened wide!

One last gift, more special than any she'd dreamed,
For there in her hand, a tiny star gleamed!

Toward the frost on the window the little girl turned,
And she smiled as she thought of all she had learned.
Though we have the world's riches, we'll find in the end,
There is nothing we'll have worth as much as a friend.

Through the Eyes of a Child

In the fresh first snowfall of the new season, the magic happens once again. With their little snowfriends, the Snowbabies return and are on every special snowflake, twinkling and winkling as they float by, gathering the starlight of a cold winter's night. But, you ask, how might I see them?

The answer is simple, yet not easy. To see the Snowbabies, you must be able to look at the world with innocence. You must be able to see Winter, in all its wondrous icy magic, through the eyes of a child.

Think back, to the very first snowfall you remember . . . the air spinning with so many twinkling snowflakes, as if the stars themselves were falling! Remember how the stars twinkled? The snow glistened? Remember the song of the North Wind?

Remember when you tried to catch a glimpse of Jack Frost as he spread his magic across the land? . . . the glittering frost pictures he left behind on the windowpane? . . . the shine of icicles? . . . the feel of cold on your nose and cheeks? . . . the crunch of snow underfoot? And when the snowflakes danced about you, remember trying to catch one so that you might keep it forever?

So, go out into the first new snowfall and look, once again, with the eyes of a child. Then and only then can you see the Snowbabies. And remember, when you see them, with each one comes the wish that a sparkle of gladness will touch your day and the Snowbaby magic will find you and surround you in every way.

Wishing on a Star

I see you, little star so bright,
High up in the frosty night.
Can you see me from where you are,
Down here *wishing on a star*?

Snowbabies©

Personal Collection of

_____

Year _____   Year _____

_____ _____   _____ _____

_____ _____   _____ _____

_____ _____   _____ _____

_____ _____   _____ _____

_____ _____   _____ _____

_____ _____   _____ _____

_____ _____   _____ _____

_____ _____   _____ _____

_____ _____   _____ _____

_____ _____   _____ _____

_____ _____   _____ _____

_____ _____   _____ _____

_____ _____   _____ _____

_____ _____   _____ _____

_____ _____   _____ _____

_____ _____   _____ _____

_____ _____   _____ _____

Year

Year

Year

_____ _____

_____ _____

_____ _____

_____ _____

_____ _____

_____ _____

_____ _____

_____ _____

_____ _____

_____ _____

_____ _____

_____ _____

_____ _____

_____ _____

_____ _____

_____ _____

_____ _____

_____ _____

_____ _____

_____ _____

_____ _____

_____ _____

_____ _____

Year

_____ _____

_____ _____

_____ _____

_____ _____

_____ _____

_____ _____

_____ _____

_____ _____

_____ _____

_____ _____

_____ _____

_____ _____

_____ _____

_____ _____

_____ _____

_____ _____

_____ _____

_____ _____

_____ _____

_____ _____

_____ _____

_____ _____

_____ _____